Theme and Variations

Theme and Variations

Vanessa Horn

Chapeltown Books

British Library Cataloguing in Publication Data

A Record of this Publication is available from the British Library

ISBN 978-1-910542-51-4

This edition published 2020 by Chapeltown Books
Manchester, England

CONTENTS

Introduction

Why write a flash fiction collection based on music? Because...

Music is such an important part of life. It's a way of expressing feelings and emotions as well as being an escape from the extremes of life.

Music is everything – from providing a source of entertainment to offering a lifeline for those in need.

Most people have been affected by music. It could be a song which transports you to a different era, place or mood, or an instrumental piece which can make you cry, laugh, or ponder the meaning of life.

Music can say many things to many people. This book is for everyone who has music in their lives – externally or internally.

Beyond the Lights

"Worlds outside our own," I repeated. "In what sense?"

Lily looked up from her guidebook. "It doesn't elaborate. Maybe in the spectrum of colours. The variety, perhaps?"

I gazed around me and saw a blur with no meaning. Of course, this was only my perspective. I'm sure everyone else in our group was admiring the Reykjanes Peninsula with perfect twenty-twenty vision. I sighed.

Lily squeezed my arm. "I'm sure you'll be able to see the lights, Tom. The guidebook says the colours can be exceptionally bright."

I smiled at her optimism. It was one of the things I loved about her. "With luck. And Lily, thank you."

She leant closer. "For?"

"You know – the planning. Sorting. Stuff."

"Mmm." She wasn't great at expressing her feelings either. "Anyway, shush now – keep watching."

We watched. Waited. Minutes passed, possibly an hour. Then suddenly, just as I was beginning to lose heart, I made out a very faint glow. Rising. As I watched, squinting and holding my breath, the light expanded, taking on a greenish cast, and then, incredibly, the skies began to move into contours. Into shapes. These swayed left then right, undulating like wayward items of laundry set free from a washing line, before scattering into tiny pieces which, one by one, enlarged and soared to all junctions of the sky.

I turned my head, following first one then another, marvelling at their vibrancy as they danced across the skies. Then, incredibly, they grew so close that now I could distinguish their forms, their outlines. Women. Women on horseback. Armoured women.

Suddenly, I heard the call of music. Voices? Violins? I was unsure. There was no distinction in ambience or resonance – just, rather oddly, an overpowering sense of yearning. A hungering. Then, amplified with the addition of trumpets, the music mood-shifted into a triumphant and stirring melody, urging and immediate. The warriors responded by guiding their horses together in one united group. Twisting south, they raced across the sky, their spears, armour and helmets glinting and flashing. Lighting up the heavens – mission bound.

It was only when the last few women disappeared into the topmost of the skies I realised the group was not alone. Behind their vibrancy and determination followed the bowed figures of uniform-clad, war-fatigued men – their shared bearing one of lassitude. Defeat. They were being led, but where?

I turned to Lily. Perhaps she could make more sense of what was happening. She put an arm around me. "I'm so sorry it was a no-show, Tom, but maybe we'll see the lights tomorrow night."

I frowned. But then, watching the last of the soldiers disappearing from view, I felt myself smiling as I realised I didn't need an explanation. Not now. *Worlds outside our own.*

A Question of Timing

David paused in his morning ablutions and peered into the misted mirror. As anticipated, the Darkness peered back at him; always present, there was no reason to expect it to be otherwise. He sighed.

Then, ensuring every towel was hanging rose-pattern outwards as required, he left the bathroom. Slowly made his way downstairs, his slippered feet *flip-flopped* on each step. Towards the kitchen. Towards Dorothy.

She didn't look up as he entered. Instead, she huffed then grunted, "Your breakfast's burnt."

David sat down heavily. "It doesn't matter." He took a quick bite of the charcoaled toast, trying, without success, not to grimace.

His wife shrugged. "Your fault. How long does it *take* to have a shower?"

Knowing no answer was required, David crunched the last mouthful with relief and then rose from the table.

Moving through to the small utility room – Toby at his heels – he changed his slippers for outdoor shoes and retrieved his terrier's lead. David clipped it on securely and turned back to Dorothy. He spoke softly, "Won't be long," then left the house.

As he shut the small wooden gate firmly behind him, David felt his shoulders begin to loosen and his heartbeat reduce into a more peaceable rhythm. The Darkness was still present. That never went away.

Looking down at the small dog, he smiled sadly. "No way to live, is it, lad?"

9

In response, Toby cocked his leg against the nearby lamppost, urinating abundantly.

"Exactly," murmured David, waiting patiently before walking on.

Down the quiet street and towards the churchyard. The usual routine. *It isn't an unpleasant morning, not for October. Sunny but with a hint of a nip. A bit like Dorothy when we first met, forty-odd years ago. A girl who knew her own mind, did her own thing. Didn't need a man, either.*

David, immediately captivated by Dorothy's free and outgoing spirit, persuaded her otherwise. Eventually. Now, and certainly not for the first time, he wondered whether he shouldn't have... Maybe then she wouldn't have grown so bitter. So vindictive.

I was so taken by her free spirit. So outgoing. So unlike me. Well, they say opposites attract. Still I persuaded her – eventually. But... maybe I should have left her to do her own thing. Perhaps she wouldn't have become so bitter then. Vindictive even.

But that hadn't been the case.

I didn't stand in her way. I encouraged her in everything – her career, her hobbies, her life. It's not my fault she lost interest in everything. Her animosity isn't my doing so why do I feel so often that it is?

David and Toby turned into the entrance to the churchyard, the latter sniffing enthusiastically at the half-sunken gravestones lying either side of the path. David stopped to look at the notice board. There they were – the yellowing coffee morning announcements, circa 2012, and handwritten postcards advertising babysitting, lawn-mowing and the like. Nothing new.

Ready to move on, he suddenly heard a noise from inside the church. Some sort of clang or clank? He waited. Moments later, the sound was repeated and, with sudden recognition, he nodded. "The bells, Toby – someone's got them working at last."

Deciding to investigate, he pushed open the heavy door and stepped inside. Blinking at the dimness, he eventually spotted a small group of men standing in a semi-circle at the far end of the church, holding vertically hanging ropes of varying thickness.

"Come to join us?" A stout man indicated the unmanned rope by his side.

David hesitated. "Well, I – "He glanced down at Toby, unsure about the protocol of dogs in churches.

The man grinned. "Bring him in, he looks obedient enough. I'm Nev, by the way."

After only a moment of hesitation, David complied, heading down the aisle towards the group.

After introductions were made by David and the others – Bill, Pete, Steve and Mark – Nev explained that he'd instigated the get-together. "I've wanted to start a campanology group for a while now, but had to get the bells checked out first."

"Nev's the only one who knows what he's doing," added Steve. "The rest of us are novices."

David felt his interest stirring. "So, do you... would you... be looking for another regular member, do you think? To join your group?"

"Definitely," Nev replied. He passed over the spare rope. "Here."

After instructing Toby to sit, David gingerly took the rope and moved into place in the line of men. Listened carefully as Nev went through the bell-ringing techniques. Apparently, it was not just a case of holding the rope correctly but you needed to move with and catch it at exactly the right time.

David nodded to himself. *Timing, that's what it's all about.*

"Time for you to have a go now, Dave," concluded Nev, after several minutes of instruction.

As he began to pull on the rope, David experienced an unanticipated and unfamiliar sensation of power. Control. Without warning, barely acknowledged sparks of pent-up frustration flew from his consciousness, down his arms and into the rope.

Then, as he continued to pull, the Darkness materialised around him, merging and augmenting these feelings. It expanded like uncontrollable shaving foam, travelling with the momentum of the ringing until – finally – it broke free, rising up, up, up to the rafts of the ceiling. Momentarily halted by the wooden beams, it then narrowed to a slit and pierced a small hole in the roof. Slid easily through and dissipated into the sky.

Now the Darkness had gone, Dave could spy a speck of blue sky peeping through the hole in the roof. New. Fresh. Unsullied.

It's hope. Just a little, but enough.

He smiled, feeling the relief spreading through his body, pore by pore, vein by vein.

With hope, he knew he would find the courage to do what he needed to do.

Life Music

I startle out of my daydream as *Yesterday* ceases – mid-verse – then lurches into dark, classical music – Wagner, possibly, or Tchaikovsky? Whatever, it's abrupt. Unexpected. An omen. So… what exactly is it warning me about?

I check around the train. Everything seems normal. Nothing remotely dangerous or threatening amongst the small groups of morning-sleepy Tube commuters. Hmm… Must be yet another blip in the system. That's three bloody times in the past week.

I sigh. However, within moments, my Beatles compilation suddenly resumes, this time with *Yellow Submarine*. A relatively short-lived glitch this time then.

As I leave the station, striding along the streets until I reach the office, the music slides into smooth jazz as usual, soothing and preparing me for the day ahead. I sit down at my desk, grinning as I notice Dan head-banging as he works across the room – each to his own, I guess. My workmate acknowledges my arrival with a mock salute and a grin before he turns back to his screen.

Right, on with the spreadsheets. Ah, the mellow tones of Diana Krall, now this is why I signed up for *Life Music*. That and the cheap(ish) rates for us guinea pigs. And, yes, I guess there's bound to be the occasional glit – Oh hell, there it goes again! *Beethoven's Fifth* this time, the strings carving out their initial motif, foreboding and brooding. Each note etching itself into my brain, attempting to destroy my concentration. Bloody hell! That's it, I'm going to the nerve centre straight after work to get it sorted. There's no way I can function effectively amidst this racket.

Meanwhile, though, I refuse to yield to the malfunction. I can't risk a decrease in my productivity. So, ignoring the threatening violins and menacing basses, I focus instead on the screen, determined to get the spreadsheet finished before lunchtime. However, as if in retaliation to being unheeded, the music intensifies. Double basses and cellos are scraped ferociously – an odd, abrasive sound – as if they're trying to escape their surroundings.

For God's sake, how can I – *Crack!* The strident sound shatters my focus and I swing my gaze upwards to see the heavy light fitting begin its launch.

Towards me.

Theme and Variations

Silenzio

Emily looks down at her baby, her sweat-streaked face creasing into worry. "Why isn't he crying?"

The midwife smiles and pats her arm. "Don't worry, Mrs Benson, we've checked him and everything's as it should be. You have a lovely little boy."

"But he's so quie—"

Alex kisses his wife. "He's perfect, love. Well done."

Detache

"Come on Lucas, say 'Mummy'. Mu – mmy."

Lucas looks up at Emily quizzically, before returning to his drawing.

Emily peers down at the page. It's as if he's been conducting an orchestra with his blue crayon and paper – up, down, up, down… Little disjointed lines, irregular in spacing, strangely tessellated. Rhythmical.

She blinks back her tears. Surely Lucas should be babbling and chattering like other toddlers of his age. In comparison to her friends' children, her own son seems… distant. Withdrawn, even. She sighs. Maybe, as Alex says, Lucas will catch up in his own time. Although he hasn't said it for a while…

Dissonante

"Of course we'll continue to take him, Mrs Benson," Miss Paulson smiles.

"He's a lovely boy. Really, it's just that he doesn't seem to be getting a lot out of nursery. On the social side, that is."

She glances over at Lucas and Emily follows her gaze. In the corner, facing the wall, her little boy is tracing shapes in the air in front of him with his finger.

"But he seems happy enough. In his own little world," responds the teacher.

Emily frowns. "He does that at home as well. It's almost as if he's responding to something the rest of us can't hear." She takes a deep breath, then confides, "I think… I think I might take him back to the doctor."

Drammatico

Dr Harris shuffles her papers. "Well, there are more tests to run, but essentially Lucas *is* capable of speaking. His vocal chords are perfectly normal – there is no physical reason why he can't talk."

Alex leans forward in his chair. "So why doesn't he then?"

Emily places a hand on her husband's arm before addressing the clinician. "Do you think the reason why he's not speaking is emotional or psychological?"

The doctor frowns slightly. "Well, it's difficult to say… If it were selective mutism then we'd expect Lucas to be talking in certain circumstances – at home for example. The fact that he has never spoken makes him unusual. However, it's reassuring he's reaching the other goalposts for his age. It seems he just doesn't see the need to talk."

Emily looks at Alex. He rubs his jaw, stubble grizzling like sandpaper.

Epifania

"So he's listening to Mr Smith playing the piano?" Emily wedges her mobile under her ear so she can continue pushing the shopping trolley.

Mrs Jenkins sounds excited. "Yes, Mrs Benson, he's absolutely mesmerised by it. Anyway, I just thought I'd let you know…"

Emily nods vigorously, forgetting she can't be seen by the infant school teacher. "Yes, thank you – thank you so much."

Commosso

"You want to buy a what?" Alex sounds confused at the end of the phone.

Emily exhales. "Look, just go with me on this one, Lex – please. Meet me in town in half an hour. We'll go to that big music shop on the High Street, I want it to be at home before we pick Lucas up from school."

Codetta

Lucas enters the living room, then runs over to the second-hand piano against the wall. Sitting on the stool, he reaches tentatively towards the keys.

Presses one, then another – carefully, methodically – then tries different combinations of notes, some discordant, some melodious. In a matter of minutes, he picks out a recognisable tune in one hand, then combines this melody with accompanying chords in the other.

"That TV theme…" whispers Emily from the doorway, from where she and Alex are watching.

Alex shakes his head. "Yes, but how does he know the sequence of the notes – the patterns, the rhythms?"

"I really don't know." Emily smiles. "But it doesn't matter. He's found a way to communicate."

Accelerando

"I'm pleased to say this year's Fairfield's Finest award goes to Lucas Benson from Year One for his beautiful piano playing in assemblies. It's hard to believe Lucas has only been playing for a short while. He's achieved so much so quickly. Well done, Lucas."

Lucas leaves his classmates sitting cross-legged on the floor and climbs the steps to the small stage. After accepting his trophy and certificate from the headmistress, he glances into the audience, locates his parents and smiles.

"Aww, he's proud of himself," whispers Emily.

Alex smiles back. "Not as proud as we are. Our music boy."

Dawn Awakening

An hour until sunrise. Silence. Claire wanders down the derelict street, eyes focused on the pavement, where the relinquished debris of the night drifts and meanders. Above her, streetlamps flicker, seeming uncertain as to when the darkness will end.

Claire walks on. Unseeing. Uncaring. Until she reaches the bridge. She stops. Lifts her eyes briefly to the skies and then, overwhelmed by the expanse, lowers them again. Shadowy water, mysterious and broody. Depths of uncertainty and ambiguity.

She sighs. Reaches into her pocket for her phone in order to replay Joel's duplicitous, conclusive message. To see whether doing so will make any difference to her feelings. Her confusion. She thinks probably not, yet an inner compulsion drives her to listen again. But then, just as she is about to press play, a soft chirruping catches her attention and she pauses.

It's an unseen bird singing tree-wards, warbling piano-soft quavers then semi-quavers. A sound like water, trickling and soothing. Claire listens, letting the music run over and below her. Through her.

After a while, the bird's efforts are joined by a louder, more strident tone; a bigger bird, she assumes. She hears a long drawn-out trill, and then a modulation.

The melody is taken up, doubled in volume, and followed by another motif, now sung by several birds: *Do it, do it, do it.* With heartbeat precision, bird by bird adds to the symphony of song, supplementing and enhancing the textures and volume of the music.

Claire lifts her eyes as the singing intensifies and the sky is slowly brush-painted in colour – the myriad of sounds and shades adding to the individual portrait of the unfolding day. She smiles, decision made.

Lifting her arm, she throws her phone into the water far below, nodding as it hits the surface with a satisfying splat before merging into the murkiness. Gone.

Straight Talking

I pause outside the open door, placing my keys in my briefcase and re-arranging my papers. Psyching myself up, really. Silly, I know, but I always need a few moments before I go in. Okay… I'm ready.

I enter the room, walking over to the white-haired man in his wheelchair. "Good afternoon, George, how are you today?"

Slowly, he turns his head from the direction of the TV. Blinks at me. Trying to place who I am? I touch his shoulder gently.

"It's me – Hannah? I visit you every few days or so."

His face creases into a smile. Finally, he nods. "Hannah."

My heartbeat quickens – he remembers! *This time*. I move to sit beside him, resting my folder on my lap.

He looks at it. "You've brought…?" He stops, seeming to have lost the words.

"The photos, yes. They're here."

He looks thoughtful. "A long and eventful story."

Ah, those are the words I used last time about his life. A good sign. I take a photo from the folder. "Shall we start from the time when your family was evacuated to the farm at Forestside?"

We look down at the grainy black and white image showing a short, plump woman surrounded by four boys of varying heights. I turn the photo over and read out the names on the back: "George, David, Trevor and Ronald. You and your brothers in 1940."

George turns away. "George was the man of the house when his father went to fight. He had to look after his mum and the boys."

I study the younger George more closely. Unlike his siblings, he looks serious, unsmiling. "How did you feel about that?"

George turns back. "He had to stay up late each night. His mother didn't like to sit alone in the evenings." He frowns, his face creasing into furrows.

He's upset? I decide to move things on, taking out a different photo. "What about school? That's where you met Grace, wasn't it, on the bus travelling there?"

His smile returns, his eyes glazing into a rheumy brown. "George and Grace sat on the back seat together. They, they…" He pauses.

I wait a few moments then try to help. "Fell in love?"

He smiles shyly before reaching over to the folder and taking out another photo – George as a teenager.

We consider the image. There's a huge difference between the tall upright figure in the photo and the emaciated George of now. I glance at the now George; he is staring at his younger self, his expression serious.

I keep my voice soft. "1959, just before National Service came to an end. Were you excited about going to sea?"

George exhales softly, then takes the photo and inspects it closely. "No fighting, though. That was before. He didn't fight."

"Yes, that's right – the war was over by then. You stayed in the Navy for two years, didn't you? Before coming back home."

George's expression seems to darken a little.

I hope his attention isn't wandering back to the unreachable. I bite my lip. Maybe it's time.

"George? I thought we could try listening to a piece of music this week. Jazz music." I wait, holding my breath. I don't know exactly how he – or I, for that matter – will feel, listening to this particular piece.

"Jazz music."

Good, he's still with me. But will he know what the music means? Will it reach him? Well… it's got to be worth trying. Quickly, I rummage in my bag, bringing out an iPod and speaker. My finger trembling, I press play.

As the sound of violins fill the room, followed by the first few words of Ray Charles's *Georgia*, I watch George. But his face is expressionless, almost as if he's switched off. From today. From me. Why now – this moment? After all, I know this song was an important part of his life.

Okay, keep calm, it doesn't matter. Maybe another song. Or another time.

But then I sense a small movement and notice George is tapping his finger on the side of the chair. Just a tiny, barely noticeable pat, but it's in time and rhythmical. He's responding!

I turn the volume up slightly and watch him in my peripheral vision, not wanting to jinx things with any sudden movement or reaction to his movements. As Ray Charles reaches the second verse, I notice George close his eyes, a small smile on his face.

The realisation he's enjoying this brings me such pleasure I have difficulty in stopping myself from running to get someone – a nurse, a doctor, anyone! – to share the sensation. But no, I just need to enjoy the moment, so I lean back in the comfortable chair, and then, like George, I close my eyes. Surprisingly, it only takes a couple of moments to lose myself in the wistful theme; the lyrics and melodies which I imagine are nearly as familiar to me as they are to George. The memories...

Car journeys with the windows wound down and the stereo blasting out. That hot summer when it never seemed to rain... The cloudless hazy sky which signified freedom and opportunity...

As the last words of the song fades away, I sigh and open my eyes.

George stops his tapping and he blinks a few times before turning to me.

I touch his hand gently. "Do you remember that song?"

He smiles. I'm pretty sure he remembers. Well, as sure as I can be. Suddenly, he laughs. "I remember singing it at the pub."

Wow – he's talking about himself in the first person! That's the first time since... well, since.

He seems to be waiting for an answer, so I reply. "Yes you did..."

I take his hand before continuing. "...Dad."

Distraction

Standing with her back to the orchestra, Genevieve acknowledges the audience, recognising their expectation and anticipation. She closes her eyes, breathing in the heady aura and relishing the power. The control. Inhale. Exhale. Inhale. Exhale.

But she knows she needs to start the journey so, opening her eyes, and with the slightest acknowledgement to the conductor beside her – *it's time* – she touches bow to violin. A caress.

Now barely aware of the audience, held-breath and programme-still in their seats, she sings out the first note, a resonant and vibrant F. Sonorously, she sustains this until, at the last possible moment, she slides into an E. Then a D, another E, and back to F.

As she adds note to note, Genevieve gradually quickens the pace, semi-quavers keeping in time with her heartbeat, until the melody flows unassisted, herself now a vehicle for the music which rises higher and higher. Playfully, she teases an early climax, continuing to cascade upwards, but then – so near to the summit – dampens the passion, targeting a portentous B-flat – a B-flat which now energises the orchestra into response. Into the music.

Immediately, soldier and legion united, the music soars stereophonically through the large concert hall, climbing to the rafters and then, with nowhere to seep, inflates, like expanding foam, into every unfilled space: a waterfall of diatonic, chromatic, arpeggiated notes.

Genevieve breathes every one, relinquishing some quickly and retaining others with wistful longing. Individually they are vital, a part of her: a cell, a whirl, a gene. While she willingly surrenders them for now, she knows they will return later, like wayward children running back to their mother at the end of an afternoon playtime. An inevitable return for, ultimately, every note belongs to her only.

Although she knows the moment is fleeting, that it cannot last any more than a moment, she, as always, loses herself in the music, refusing to think of before, of after. She is the music: the music is her. That's the way it is. How it should be.

Therefore, as she plays the final note of the movement, she is uncushioned and unprotected for the shock of the return: the return to physicality.

The door creaks open and a smiling, uniform-clad, middle-aged woman enters the room. "It's only me. Are you ready for your bath now, Genevieve? Sarah and I are helping you tonight."

With the music gone, Genevieve recoils inwardly, unable to express herself with voice or movement. Although it has been over three years now, she still wonders whether her mind might explode at any time with the frustration, the fear, the indignity of this illness.

Suddenly, a bell rings from the hallway. The older woman hesitates and then pats Genevieve's arm gently. "I'll see to that and then I'll be back – won't be long, love."

A reprieve. She returns the bow to the strings and nods to the conductor. Smiles within her heart as she begins the second movement...

Shade Sensations

I was eight or nine when I realised words couldn't be trusted.

It was a warm summer day just before breakfast when my mother, limited in pleasantries, not to mention cavalier in manner, announced, "Your father has moved out."

The words were simple but the colours I felt were not. No, these took the form of pulsating, vibrant shades of red, as blistering as the centre of our open fire, flames licking at log edges, waiting to erupt and scald any innocent passer-by.

It was then I recognised it was colours, and not words, which told the truth.

With colours, there were just enough shades to gain every nuance and sensation you needed. No more, no less. Example: next door's terrier, Lucy. The russet brown which emanated from her told me she was ready to play. And Smokey-Smudge, my lop-eared rabbit – when I sensed his delicate shade of pink, I knew he was hungry or lonely. Animals were easy.

My peers, too, really, once they'd established I wasn't going to interrupt or argue with them anymore. Their changing sense-colours allowed me to quickly gauge their moods, their auras. Inevitably, I became popular; the girl who acquiesced. Albeit silently.

Of course, it was the adults who made the most fuss about my elective mutism. After once branding me a chatterbox, the teachers rightly – but not for the reasons they perceived – blamed my silence on the abrupt departure of my father. Immediately, they went all out, hauling in the Ed Psych and every other official they could lay their hands on.

Considering how many times I'd previously been reprimanded for nattering, you'd have thought they'd have appreciated the sudden peace. Encouraged it, even. But no, they had to investigate, to try to resolve the 'problem'. Looking back, I suppose, in a strange way, I enjoyed this attention, appreciating my new status of mysterious, never-speaking child.

Being silent had other advantages too. At home each evening, when Mother finally exhausted her new-found cleaning regime, we tended to sit together companionably, watching TV or just staring into the fire. It was almost as if we had a fresh understanding. One which was undemanding. Peaceful.

Did that mean my father had been the instigator of all previous arguments and rows? Probably not; it could've just been the combination of the two of them – mismatched personalities maybe. And... perhaps I had my part to play in the irregular dynamics. Who knew? But, whatever the reasoning, I appreciated the new serenity.

Communicating wasn't a problem. Not while I used my colour palette. I thought in colours, dreamt in colours. Expressed myself by using colours, not just in my paintings (although I did these daily) but colours in my head as well. It was a new life. A different life. It worked for me. It didn't let me down.

Until one day, time later. Again, it was morning and I was walking to school. Somewhat friendless by this stage – after all, I had been mute for a few months now and the novelty of a silent me had worn off – I was by myself, dawdling, daydreaming.

Then I noticed the small tabby cat wandering along the pavement. Simultaneously, I sensed the colours around him. Shades of red, as before. Danger. Menace. I didn't recognise why at first.

Not until he neared the edge of the pavement and I saw he was going to cross the road. The busy, traffic-laden road.

I opened my mouth to shout a warning. But my lazy vocal chords resisted the effort after so many days of silence, emitting nothing more than a half-hearted strangled-sounding moan. A pathetic and diluted grey – no use to anyone. Not least a traffic-oblivious cat.

My heart pumping faster now, – I tried again. With much more vigour. And with a deep, rich black: anxiety and desperation. This time, although not quite a shout, my voice was louder – "Stop!" – and the cat heard me.

He looked around. Then, with a swish of his tail, darted back the way he had come, towards the hedges away from the traffic. Away from danger.

Legs suddenly wobbly, I sank onto the pavement, watching the animal slink into the distance, oblivious to anything but himself.

After that, I got it. I understood more than I had before. Most importantly, I realised I couldn't change the way things were, and certainly not when I was still a child, that my self-enforced silence made no difference to anyone, least of all me. I didn't know then that a lot of what is said isn't always what's meant. Why would I?

After I'd heard my voice again, there didn't seem to be any point in continuing my mutism. Don't know whether it was the cat incident or just that I had come to terms with what had happened, even though I still didn't know the details of my father leaving home to live with another woman.

Maybe I had an inkling that lies – black or white – can be the way people get through things. To pat things down a little, as it were. So I continued to speak again. Hesitantly and so softly only the closest in proximity could hear me. Understand me. But it was a start, I suppose. A re-emerging into humanity.

However, I never did trust words again, even years later. Although I continued to speak throughout the rest of my childhood, I still relied predominantly on colours for knowledge and intuition.

They told the absolute truth. Always.

Synaesthesia

I was eleven when I found out I wasn't normal. That experiencing music with all your senses rather than just hearing was unusual. Bizarre, even.

Before then, I assumed the huge, reeking creatures which I flinched from during *The Farmer in the Dell* were encountered by everyone. My wincing at dust-clouds and pounding hoofs in *Camptown Races*? Part and parcel of the music, like fish accompanying chips. So, I didn't question my responses – didn't talk about them. Didn't realise I was different.

Until that morning in assembly. The Head had chosen to play the *1812 Overture* as we sat, waiting. The music started and I smiled, watching pure-white doves fly gently around our heads. But, just seconds later, as an erupting volcano emerged from nowhere, flooding the hall with scalding lava and red-tipped flames, I jumped up. Screamed.

When I was asked for an explanation, my stuttered but honest response was derided. Ridiculed. As if I could see volcanoes in a piece of music! Absolute rubbish! Detention after school.

And my peers? Well, safe to say, this episode didn't do a lot for my popularity. No-one likes a weirdo...

But at lunchtime, a girl I knew slightly – Beth – came over with her tray. "Okay to sit here?"

I shrugged. Things couldn't get any worse.

We sat silently for a few minutes before she spoke again.

"Anna, when you screamed—"

I stood. I'd had enough of ridicule and embarrassment for today.

"No – don't go! It's just, well, I wanted to say I sometimes see pictures in music too. Just pictures but… it's similar, isn't it?"

I sat down again, my mind whirling. Knew it was a big deal for her to admit this. Feeling the tension dissolve from my shoulders and neck, I exhaled. Then smiled. "Yes. It is."

Notes of Resentment

It's normal for the music to arrive gently in the mornings.

Sometimes *Clair de Lune* tiptoes into her consciousness; a soft prelude into daylight with arpeggios caressing the keys. Other days, it's the *E-Flat Major Nocturne*, opening with its legato piano melody scaling graceful upward leaps. Gentle. Soothing.

But not today. No, today Megan is jolted awake with the pound of C-sharp octaves in the form of Liszt's *Hungarian Rhapsody*.

Startling and forceful, fortissimo chords charge into her awareness with purpose and clarity, determined not to be ignored. She waits, desperately hoping the music will quickly subside into the soothing timbres she is used to, allowing her to begin her day.

No. The music thunders on, remorseless. Disturbing. She frowns, confused, for the morning melodies always reflect her state of mind from the previous day. Without fail. After Ben's marriage proposal last night, she'd have expected joyful trills, uplifting cadenzas and whimsical riffs this morning. Most fitting of all would have been a rendering of the *Wedding March*. Not this… cacophony.

Crash! The piece finishes. Megan holds her breath, waiting. Hoping. Perhaps now…? A brief pause of optimism and then – oh God – a strident military march springs into life. Piercing trumpets in their highest range.

She winces, instinctively wanting to block her ears with her hands, but knowing there's no point; the music is, as always, internal. Within her consciousness. It's been there ever since she can remember – a constant companion throughout childhood, adolescence, and now adulthood. More familiar to her than Ben, even, who, despite making her heart dance and her senses soar, has only been in her life for the past four years.

She glances at her phone – 7.15 – and sighs. Inching herself out of bed, she slips on her dressing gown and slowly makes her way downstairs. Despite the hectic quavers and unreliable semi-quavers which continue to ravage her brain, one notion pushes its way right to the forefront of the clamour: work.

Usually the music sustains her through the day, calming and comforting her as she teaches, but there's no way she can face thirty excitable seven year olds with this raging battle of notes exploding in her mind. She taps out a text to the head teacher: *struck down with a migraine, hopefully back tomorrow.*

Then a further worry shrieks out from the discordancy. *Will* she be able to return to work the next day? Suppose this type of music continues to torment her for the rest of her life? She'd never be able to function normally again. Megan's skin tingles with anxiety and waves of panic spike the tiny hairs on her arms.

As the orchestral dissonances continue to rain sharp tacks into the inner recesses of her brain, she tries to think of a way – *any* way – of coaxing the music around and restore it to its normal harmonious melodies. Perhaps she can replace the offensive sounds with something more tuneful. One of Brahms's lullabies, maybe?

Okay… Focus, Megan. Auralise the notes… a pianissimo C then a gentle trickle of harmonies…

It's no good. The music seems antagonised by her futile attempts, crescendoing into an ear-splitting shriek of jagged triplets in retaliation.

Megan gasps, immediately regretting the small but painful movement. She wills herself to concentrate. There must be a *reason* for this happening. Surely the music wouldn't turn against her after all this time without a motive? So… perhaps the way forward is finding out *why* it's putting her through this torment? Then she could find a solution.

She closes her eyes, intent on blocking out everything but the music. *Go with the notes, don't fight them…* Immediately, the volume decreases a little – not much but enough for Megan to allow her thoughts to be heard more easily.

Okay… Are you trying to tell me something?

Immediately, the notes soar in pitch, quickly accelerating into frenzied heights, and she flinches, realising she has found her explanation. But… if it's a warning, what is it of? She can't think of any hazardous endeavour she's due to undertake in the near future. Unless…

One life-changing aspect – the *only* element which has changed recently – is the intensifying of her relationship with Ben. Culminating in his proposal… No! Surely it can't be that which has altered her music's mood? Or can it? Is the music resentful?

As Megan considers this, piano notes suddenly auralise – Debussy's *First*

Arabesque – the melodies washing over her like the first signs of spring after a particularly hard winter. Ah…

She groans, understanding, unwelcome as it is, she now has the answer.

"You're jealous?" she murmurs, hardly able to believe it.

How could anyone – let alone the music – disapprove of Ben: his loving smile, generous actions, impulsive ideas? Couldn't she have both – music (the agreeable version) *and* a husband? But, even as she considers this, she knows what the answer is. Knows there's no way she can live a normal life with this turmoil in her head. She has no choice.

"You, you… win," she mutters reluctantly.

In response, the melodies and harmonies purr gently, smug and appeased.

Sighing heavily, Megan picks up her mobile and locates her fiancé's number. And, after she presses *call*, the music slips effortlessly into a light waltz, dancing merrily – *triumphantly*? – as she waits for him to pick up.

Food for Thought

I normally ignore the station vending machine when I travel by train, reading, or re-reading the stories inside my thoughts instead. Not from any traditionalist objections to the machines themselves – I think the dispenser concept is a brilliant idea – it's just that on my meagre income I must economise.

However, today I need a distraction, something to keep my anxieties at bay. I require diversion. Entertainment. So I pause at the large orangey-red structure to consider the options, reading each suggestion with scrupulous impartiality. Horror? Romance? Thriller? Historical? Hmmm. My finger hovers over the options. Hard to decide when my whole being is effervescing with interview nerves.

I sigh and press the *Surprise me!* button. God knows, the dispenser has to make a better choice of fiction than I can. After a few seconds of whirring and grumbling – from the machine, not me – several sheets of paper emerge.

Grabbing them eagerly, I board the train and find myself a seat. Begin reading.

Life is too short to dwell on indecision... I stop, lift my gaze and stare out of the window. Mmm, that's true. I've been accused of over-thinking many a time. Obsessing. Regretting. Procrastinating. I smile as I realise I'm doing exactly that right now. I return to the story.

...and I've found this out the hard way although, fortunately, not before it was too

*late. In telling my story, perhaps I can help you, the reader, even if it's in choosing to **make** decisions – sometimes the hardest part of all.*

I nod, thinking of all the angst I'd gone through in just deciding to attend this job interview.

In fact, I'd picked up my mobile several times to cancel. I'd deliberated. I wasn't right for the job… I wouldn't get it anyway… it was too far to travel every day… You name it, I had an excuse for it. I'm not sure why I was so reluctant to go for the position. Anyway, finally, my friends and family had persuaded me to give it a try.

"It's a useful experience just going for the interview," Mum said, probably exasperated by my uncertainty.

Anyway, so much for this being a diversion from my nerves. I read on, finally feeling myself being drawn away from my current situation and into the words. It's a sort of rite of passage-type story – I suppose you'd classify it as realistic fiction, or maybe chick-lit, I'm not exactly sure. A young woman – Jess – who is about my age, is on her way to audition for a place at the Royal College of Music. A physical and emotional journey, like the one I am taking today.

I smile at this. It's not often you read a story which parallels your own life. Although, unlike me, Jess *is* certain in her ambitions. Has worked towards this moment since she was a child, practising piano for hours on end to the exclusion of friends and other hobbies. So, she is on the final part of her physical journey – the Tube – when she has a strange, premonition that she shouldn't be there.

...a shiver of fear washes over me and my mind is overtaken by one thought and only one thought: get out now.

Responding to this mysterious inner voice, she disembarks at the next station, regardless of the fact she'll now have to find an alternative way to Kensington.

I stop reading. An inner voice. Wasn't that the same thing as I'd experienced when wondering about going for this interview? Or was it just nerves? With so much encouragement from other sources, I'd almost disregarded my own feelings altogether.

But... now I open my mind to my former misgivings. Why don't I want to be making this journey? Is it the job interview itself? Or something else entirely?

At this last thought, and as the train pulls into the penultimate station before mine, decision flashes over me.

Get out now.

My inner voice? I stumble to my feet and, as the door beeps before closure, I jump awkwardly down onto the platform.

Unable to believe I just did that, I turn and watch as the train accelerates away into the distance.

Okay... I still need to get to this interview. I frown as I now realise *that* didn't have anything to do with my foreboding. So, shaking myself out of my stupor, I trail out to the waiting line of taxis, and open the door of the first car.

"Could you take me to Hastings House, please?"

The young driver smiles and nods as I climb in.

But, before he can even start the engine, we both flinch as a thunderous *bang* resonates from outside. Turning to stare out of the back window, I see a large and rapidly growing cloud of smoke rising from the direction of the train track.

The track on which my train was travelling. I feel my eyes widen as I comprehend. At what had happened. At what could have happened.

Time for Change

God waved the yellowing parchment under Peter's nose. "Just how long have we been using the Seven Deadly Sins as our guidelines for entry to Heaven?"

Peter reflected. Was this one of those hypothetical questions that his Creator was so fond of posing? He took a deep breath. "Ermm… well… some time ago? Um…" He paused, biting his lip and frowning.

God nodded. "Exactly. Some time ago indeed. Since the *beginning* of time, to be precise. Therefore, the Sins are now incredibly out of date. Obviously." He indicated downwards. "Look!"

Peter squinted myopically towards earth. There appeared to be a huge party taking place: hilarity, dancing and enjoyment on a grand scale. Despite this, however, he concluded none of the Sins were being openly exhibited. Not *exactly*.

God narrowed his eyes, almost as if he'd read Peter's mind.

Which He probably had, Peter surmised, *Him being God.*

"As you can see," continued God, "humans have become crafty. Manipulative. And, as a result of this rule-bending, Heaven's being inundated with riff-raff."

"Right…" Peter replied. "*Riff-raff…*"

"So…" God spoke briskly, "I'll give you a week for the rewrite. You need to make the rules much more challenging." He turned and strode back through the gates, seemingly satisfied the situation was now under control.

Peter stared after him. Rewrite the Sins? Oh God! He groaned as he realised this task, not trouble-free by any means, would also include his vilest nightmare – an excursion to Earth.

And, worse still, the said destination would need to be a densely populated area, so he could study exactly how the riff-raff were bending the rules and entering Heaven so easily. Marvellous.

Then he shrugged. What was the point in bemoaning his fate? After all, the job had to be done, regardless of his sensitivities, so he just needed to get on with it. He deliberated over possible venues for a while. Hmmm, London's Oxford Street was probably the best location for this loathsome job. Inhaling deeply – no sense in procrastinating – he prepared to jump.

Moments later, he was gazing absently around Hyde Park (navigation had never been his strong point). Okaay. It wasn't immediately obvious what needed to be changed within the Sins. Yes, people *were* stretching the boundaries – some quite considerably – but they *were* still within the original criteria. There was no obvious adultery, stealing, etc. Therefore, they wouldn't be refused entry to Heaven when their time came. People *were* crafty.

Brows furrowed, Peter sank down onto a nearby bench. After a few moments, hearing voices, he looked up, spotting two small children a short distance away.

The smaller boy seemed to have fallen over and was crying. The other put his arm round his friend, hugging him and murmuring reassuring words.

Within seconds, the little boy's tears had ceased. Forgotten. An act of kindness had seemingly saved the day.

As the boys skipped off towards the playground, Peter was gratified – and somewhat relieved – to experience a rush of inspiration. Why did the Seven Sins *need* to be deadly? God had not specified this in his outlines, after all.

So… why not reward *good* deeds instead? Be proactive? Yes! That way, admission to Heaven could be for those people who had carried out the kindest and most considerate of deeds. Basically, riff-raff would not gain entry any longer. Sorted!

Quickly, Peter whipped out a notepad and pen from his robe pocket and began scrawling:

The Seven Benevolent Virtues:

1. Compassion…

2. Empathy…

The Earworm

It was an irksome earworm – the worst ever.

Don't get me wrong, I'd had plenty of these blighters over the years, so I certainly had the authority to categorise this one proficiently. And I was accustomed to the frustration whenever they occurred.

Many a time I'd been happily daydreaming when a well-known theme tune would suddenly pester me with its irritating jingle. Or I'd wake with an overly-influential aspect of the dawn chorus having planted the seed of a catchy phrase inside my mind. (*My toe hurts, Betty* frequently featured as one cantankerous culprit).

And, even when I'd gone to sleep with my brain blessedly empty from melodies or rhythms, I'd frequently be roused with an emergent phrase or a glissando beginning to tiptoe through my consciousness. Annoying. Exasperating.

But I'd never experienced anything like this earworm. Nothing had ever scratched at the inside of my awareness like this did, so desperate it was to externalise itself.

It first assailed me as I walked through the park on my way to work.

Don't know what set it off: could've been the whistle of the wind, the tap-tap-tap of the smartly-dressed business woman's high heels as she passed by, or the hum of distant traffic. Anything, really.

Whatever the trigger, the earworm sneaked up like an ostrich feather tickling a new-born's toes. Gently. Stealthily. Just a few notes to begin with; a low G, an F-sharp, a D – so transient I couldn't be sure of their existence. Not at first, anyhow.

But then the notes repeated themselves, also adding a couple of As and a B-flat for good measure. Confidently now, as if they considered themselves to have a right to be there. Were bidden. Invited. Then, as they frolicked their melody a third time and then a fourth, I sighed heavily, knowing this earworm wasn't going any time soon.

So I sat on a scuffed bench, preparing to spend however long it took to deal with the dilemma. Being no novice to these bothersome creatures, I naturally have a series of tried and tested techniques to hasten their removal. Some strategies take longer than others, understandably, depending on the severity of the insistence. Another factor is my strength of mind on the day I am afflicted. Fortunately, it was early morning and I felt alert. Optimistic.

I began with the obvious: the shaking of the head. Lightly at first in case it was a minor infestation, then progressing to a vigorous jarring when it became apparent it wasn't. Ignoring the curious glances of passers-by – do *they* never have earworms? – I slapped first one, then the other side of my head, hoping to jar the pesky bug out of its comfort zone. This had no effect except for a vigorous ringing joining the repetition of the notes. Double irritation.

With no success, it was time for the next stage. For this, I needed water, so I scanned the park for the nearest public toilets. Still hoping to get this nuisance cleared up in time to reach the office by nine, I set off at a brisk pace. The earworm obligingly increased its pace to match my steps. Frustrated, I slowed, stopped, and then sped up again, hoping to confuse it. No such luck – equalling every variation, it was obviously an earworm of the smartest kind. Damn it!

Thankful the lavatories were empty and I could avoid any more dubious stares, I shoved the plug in a sink and turned the cold tap on to full blast. Cupping water into my hand, I tilted my head, allowing the liquid to trickle into my right ear. Then I repeated the procedure on the other ear. Waited. But no, the notes were still making their presence felt, albeit in a gurgling, glugging fashion: G… F-sharp… D…

Despite feeling disconcerted – this last remedy usually works – I told myself to remain calm. I could overcome this earworm.

I'd got rid of them before, after all. So… I would have to resort to my third and final option – volume domination. I hadn't used this many times previously. I hadn't needed to, fortunately. When I had, I'd always experienced nasty side effects – migraines, nausea, that sort of thing. But needs must – desperate measures and all that.

I retrieved my high-tech headphones out of my briefcase and slapped them onto my ears. Leaving the Gents and sinking down on the grass outside, I turned the volume to maximum (I'd long since had the safety limit removed) and flicked the on switch.

Immediately, my ears filled with the rock music which I found so successful for earworm elimination. Thudding, banging, tuneless noises which – finally – drowned out my earworm. Thank God!

Despite knowing I was going to have worse side effects than ever before, I left the music on for a good five minutes to be on the safe side. After that, I punched the off button and flung the headphones away. Thank God that part was over! I waited. For a few seconds, all I could hear was the aftermath of the music: ringing, thumping, echoing.

But then, incredibly, the earworm returned... same notes as before, repeated over and over. Mocking. Teasing. What could I do? My mind – and ears – buzzing, I rose unsteadily.

Looked around for inspiration. It wasn't far away. A solitary workman, earmuffed and fluorescent jacket-clad, was busy with a chainsaw, cutting down a small tree nearby. A *chainsaw*...

Could I? Would I? But, as the notes continued to resonate throughout my psyche, I realised I had no choice. I groaned and started to walk over...

Those Weirdos Are Your Tribe

Wanted: enthusiastic volunteers to form an amateur band. Musical instruments provided (generously donated by Rev Smithson). No previous experience or knowledge needed. Rehearsals on Tuesday evenings, 7 p.m. at Bantley Village Hall, starting 28th March. Anybody and everybody welcome.

I peer around the wooden door, still uncertain. Is this a bad idea – am I inviting failure by even venturing out tonight? After all, it's the biggest attempt I've made towards social interaction since... well, just since. The sight I'm greeted with doesn't exactly fill me with confidence either. Small groups of people sitting around the hall chatting – some animatedly, others quietly.

I chew my lip. Then the decision is suddenly made for me as a grinning, freckled man pulls the door open from inside.

"Coming in then, love?" he invites, drawing me gently into the room (which now appears to have developed into an inferno of social revelry as far as I can ascertain).

Oh hell – I'm committed. At least for this first meeting. So, in I shamble, sitting as far back as possible. Away from the stage. The strangers. Hopefully I'll be inconspicuous here. I just need to wait it out – couple of hours, max – and then I can go home.

Home. Hmm. Not much of a sanctuary. Not anymore. But, miserable though it is, I don't have to try there. I can watch the world go by without having to be an interactive, sociable part of it.

Uninvited, Julia's words of a few days ago come back to me. "You've got to start putting your life back together, Soph, it's been two years now. You know David wouldn't have wanted…" Her voice tailed away at that point, as if she regretted initiating the conversation.

But her words hit their mark. David *wouldn't* have wanted me to hide myself away, driving off friends and associates alike with my apathy and sadness. Only Julia stuck around but it seemed even *her* empathy was wearing thin now. I'd decided, there and then, I had to do something – *anything* – no matter how I felt inside. Hence my attendance tonight.

Freckles, obviously in charge, now strides up the few steps to the small stage, positioning himself behind a table laden with musical instruments. My gaze drops to these and I take a sudden intake of breath as I'm sure I can see a u—

"Ahem." My thoughts are interrupted as Freckles clears his throat loudly. Conversations fade as he eventually gains the attention of the group, beaming around at everyone.

I take the opportunity to also gaze round, albeit surreptitiously, my curiosity hidden under my all-year-round sunglasses. So. There seems to be an eclectic mix of ages and stages here, if I'm honest. Despite myself, I smile wryly, wondering where I fit in *if* I fit in. I glance down at my old sweater, faded jeans and scuffed boots. Making an effort hadn't involved finding decent clothes to wear, or make-up, for that matter. Oh well.

Part of me acknowledged it was a shame I hadn't told Julia of my intentions; she probably would've insisted on coming with me, making the experience slightly more bearable. But no, I wanted to surprise her next time I saw her. Show that I'd listened to what she'd said.

Talking of listening, I tuned back in to what Freckles, who'd introduced himself as Alan, was saying.

"...and I'm sure you're wondering what kind of band can be formed with a group of randoms like us. Well, the answer is, I don't know..."

I raise my eyebrows as some people murmur and others laugh politely.

Freckles – Alan – grins back before continuing. "But, whatever your ability is, or isn't, I'm sure we can make some sort of music. We have a great selection of gadgets, after all," and here he waves his hand to encompass the instruments on the table, "from didgeridoos to xylophones. So – how to get started... any ideas, folks?"

The murmuring intensifies before one of the women – I vaguely recognise her as one of the dog-walkers who frequently passes by my house – stands up. "Hi, I'm Bev. Maybe the first thing to do is to see who wants to claim which instrument? Anyone want to start?"

I watch as a few people stand up, some immediately and others hesitantly. One by one, they walk up, murmur amongst themselves, then pick up their preferred choice of instrument. Now the number of objects available is reducing, I can see it clearly, sitting there shiny and green. Waiting. For me?

Alan nods at the volunteers. "Brilliant. Now perhaps the rest of us should each choose one of the instruments which are remaining to take home and try? By next session, we'll probably know whether we want to continue with it or swap."

An elderly man stands up. "My name's James. I fancy having a bash at the drum, if that's okay with everyone?"

Alan laughs, indicating that James joins him on the stage to claim his choice. Then another couple of people retrieve, respectively, the violin and ocarina.

I bite my lip. If I don't act soon, it'll be taken. I *must* do it. Now. I quickly stand, my chair rasping on the hard floor. Take a breath. "Um, I'm Sophie. I… I'd like to play the ukulele?" I pause. I *had* desperately wanted to play it when I was a child, watching old films of George Formby strumming away, but *could* I do it? The way I feel these days?

Alan seemingly has no such worries. "Sounds perfect, Sophie, seeing as there's a rather nice little uke here with your name on it." He grabs it and jumps off the stage, passing it to me.

I venture a smile. "Thanks." I grip the ukulele, which feels solid. Safe. So… I've shot myself in the foot now, to be clichéd, but – and I take a quick breath, trying to gauge how I feel – I think it'll be alright. And I think I'll be alright too. Eventually.

Contraband

"Be careful." The elderly man's words thud in my footsteps as I walk home, avoiding any interaction or eye contact. No one must suspect what I've acquired – for their sakes and mine.

Home. I scan in, my heart thudding. Not long now... Squeezing myself into the small space in the furthest corner of the room, I pray I'm right in fathoming I can't be observed here. No sensors. No cameras.

Finally, with shaking hands, I unwrap my black-market purchase from its packaging, breathing in the delicious smell of old paper before opening up the songbook.

Unheard Melody

Bleep. Bleeeeep. How am I supposed to sleep with that dratted machine squawking? It's not even a regular pattern of sounds. *That* you could get used to – it'd probably bore you into oblivion, like a well-behaved metronome. But no, this varies, sometimes producing drawn-out rallentandos, other times staccato drop-ins. And once an ominous but blessedly tranquil silence, all-too-soon broken when the nurse rushed in to reattach an errant wire. *Bleeep.*

The same nurse – Brian – appears now, brisk in efficiency and patronising in manner. "Is there anything I can get you, Andrew? Are you quite comfortable?"

I'm about to – churlishly, I know – mutter a retort but then I reconsider. "Actually, I don't suppose I could have something to help me sleep? This infernal bleeping is driving me mad."

Brian looks surprised. "Really? Your hearing must be particularly sensitive. Though… well, you're a musician, aren't you?"

"I *archive* music, yes," I reply, sounding like the prototypical grumpy old man. *Get a grip, Andrew.* I force myself to adopt a more agreeable tone. "So, may I? Please?"

After assenting, somewhat reluctantly, Brian departs, returning minutes later with two small pills and a glass of water. I gulp down the medication and try to readjust the sterile yet inexplicably scratchy bedding. Now for some much-needed sleep.

My optimism is short-lived. I remain awake, still unable to ignore the bleeping. For *bleep's* sake; surely I should be able to overcome this annoyance without physically ripping out the tubes and wires? *Bleep.*

Right, I *can* surmount this. After all, I'd managed to block out practically everything since I was a teenager years ago. Arguing parents, teasing peers... no-one really bothered me. I focused on my music and that was all I needed.

Of course, that was when it was all new to me. Unknown harmonies that would, in time, become old friends. Now there are no surprises. I know exactly where each note is heading – know precisely where it will swoop or soar. But I still can – and do – appreciate these familiar pieces.

Yet... it doesn't stop me yearning for that thrill of anticipation I used to experience, hearing a composition for the first time. But that's never going to happen again, is it? It's not as if Bruch is going to materialise and compose one more symphony just for me. I laugh out loud, causing Brian to leave his desk and wander over to me. *Bleep.*

"Everything alright, Andrew?" he says, giving me what he probably imagines is a caring smile. "Thought you'd be asleep by now."

"You and me both," I mutter, abandoning any pretence of politeness. "Stupid pills aren't working."

"Give them time, old chap," Brian murmurs before returning to his workstation. *Bleeep.*

Time? *Time?* Well, perhaps it *is* time for me. Maybe I've done all I was meant to do. And... well, there aren't many people to hang around for, either.

No family. No friends. Except… Jake. Would I call him a friend? I'm unsure. Though I'm more receptive with him than anyone else. Forced circumstances initially; him a young college-leaver ready to step into the world of music archiving, myself plunged – unwillingly – into the role of mentor. Advisor. A situation which felt excruciatingly awkward, initially.

Until we began our work. As the first strains of Bruch's *First Violin Concerto* played out, the notes drew us into a shared language of melodies and harmonies. We worked as one, with the same aspirations; the same satisfactions. It was all about the music. *Bleeeep.*

Yet I don't expect Jake to be here as I shuffle into my twilight phase. After all, he's like me: a young Andrew. And young Andrew would've shied away from situations like this. Jake will be at work, listening to music, evaluating it, immersing himself into it. Just as I did. It's satisfying, the idea of my protégé continuing the tradition, just as I instructed him. My work complete.

However… Do I feel ready to leave the music? Have I really fulfilled all I was supposed to do? Hmm. I suppose the answer has to be in the affirmative. I've experienced all the great pieces from the period, after all; no surprises left. *Bleep.*

My thoughts are suddenly interrupted by a disturbance over by the doors. I look up, curious. *Jake.* Clutching a small rucksack, he neatly avoids Brian's inane attempts to forestall him and bounds straight over, plonking himself down on my bed. "Andrew! Have you listened to the news recently?"

I smile – that's so like him; no polite enquiries about my health or justifications as to why he hasn't come to visit before now. He's obviously on a mission and that's all that matters. I shake my head as he continues.

"Well – a manuscript's been found in Cologne – an original violin concerto by…" Here he pauses. For dramatic effect? For breath?

"Not… *Bruch*?"

He nods vigorously. "It's been verified – I didn't come before I knew it was definite, but it's Bruch's *Fourth Violin Concerto*!! The LSO played it through yesterday and I managed to get a special pass to listen to it. Also…" Another pause, this time definitely for effect. "…I obtained permission to record it for you!" He rummages in his rucksack, brings out a small headset and presents it to me.

I close my eyes, letting the magnitude of this discovery sink in. Another Bruch violin concerto to listen to for the very first time. After all these years…

After a few moments, I open my eyes and nod my thanks to Jake. He grins then leaves without a word.

I don the headphones, press play, and wait. Exhale as the music begins to soar around and within me. And now, focusing on the music singing out to me in exquisite detail, I can, finally, ignore the bleeps.

About the Author

In 2015 Vanessa's first book – a collection of short stories entitled *Eclectic Moments* – was published by Alfie Dog Fiction. This was subsequently long listed for the 2016 Edge Hill Prize. https://smarturl.it/22rs3z

Vanessa began writing for children in 2017, and two years later won the Swanwick Children's Writing Competition (in association with Writing Magazine) with *Olly's Monster Night*. Her first picture book – *Waaaaa!* – was released on 16th January 2020 by Tiny Tree Children's Books:
https://www.matthewjamespublishing.com/products/tiny-tree/waaaaaa

Vanessa's most recent achievements are the inclusion of her story *Christingle* in *The Best of Cafelit 8* (Chapeltown Books) – https://smarturl.it/coomma – and being chosen as a finalist with her flash fiction, *Space*, in the Scottish Arts Trust Short Story Awards:
https://www.storyawards.org/2019-story-awards

Also By Chapeltown Books

140 x 140
by Gill James

This anthology of women's fiction, this collection of very short stories, some might say a flash collection, is thought-provoking and each story is based upon a tweet. Except that each piece is 140 words long and not 140 characters.

"In this entertaining book, Gill James chose the first picture she saw on her Twitter feed on specific dates. As the title suggests, there are 140 stories, each of 140 words. Some tales are laugh out loud funny, others thoughtful, and there are tragic stories too. Whatever your mood, you will find plenty to suit you here." *(Amazon)*

Order from Amazon:

ISBN: 978-1-910542-35-4 (paperback)
978-1-910542-36-1 (ebook)

Chapeltown Books

Paisley Shirt
by Gail Aldwin

Paisley Shirt is a fascinating collection of 27 stories that reveal the extraordinary nature of people and places. Through a variety of characters and voices, these stories lay bare the human experience and what it is like to live in our world.

"I really enjoyed every one of Gail Aldwin's perfectly-formed little stories, and was hooked from the very first one." (*Amazon*)

Order from Amazon:
ISBN: 978-1-910542-29-3 (paperback)
978-1-910542-30-9 (ebook)

Chapeltown Books

Slimline Tales
by Roger Noons

Each piece has been inspired by something seen, heard or told about. Much of what you will read is based on reality and wherever the narrative has strayed from that, it has been in order to create a story or achieve an appropriate ending.

If you have time to read this volume from cover to cover, that's fine. But if you're limited to dipping, moments here and there to read just a few words, then equally, this slim volume is for you.

Order from Amazon:

ISBN: 978-1-910542-27-9 (paperback)
978-1-910542-28-6 (ebook)

Chapeltown Books